T0383488

To Andrew Gray for sharing his passion and love of frogs and lizards with my family x

First published by the Natural History Museum, Cromwell Road, London SW7 5BD
Text and illustrations © John Hamilton, 2021
www.johnhamiltonartist.com
Layout © The Trustees of the Natural History Museum, London, 2021

ISBN 9780565095093

A catalogue record for this book is available from the British Library

10 9 8 7 6 5 4 3 2 1

Reproduction by Saxon Digital Services
Printed by Toppan Leefung Printing Limited

The girl who really really really loves Nature

John Hamilton

Published by the Natural History Museum, London

It is fair to say that Lara
and her dog Cassie love
EVERYTHING
about nature!

She wears her fox
costume because that
is her favourite animal.

Whatever the weather, she loves going for walks in the park with Cassie.

And she spends hours exploring in her garden. She looks under rocks for bugs.

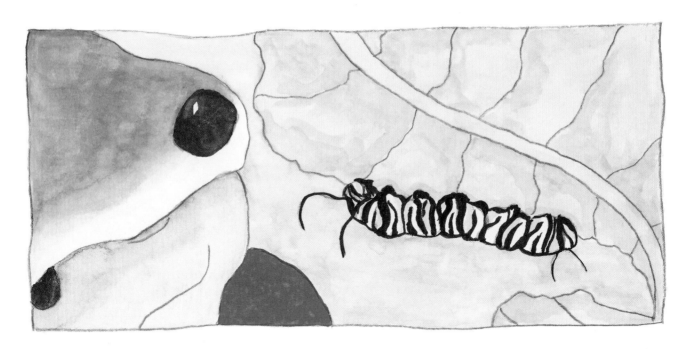

She searches leaves for caterpillars.

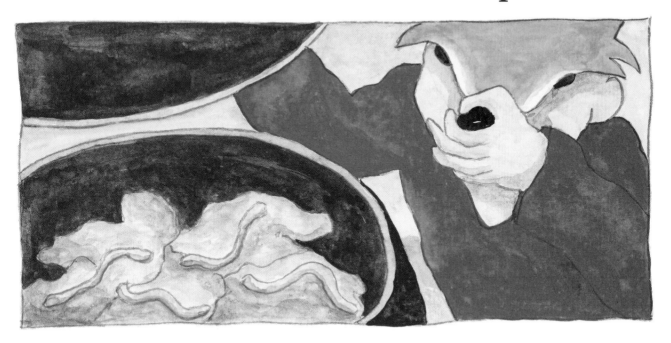

She even looks in the smelly
compost bin for WORMS.

She loves snails, which she collects in her
pockets. She often comes home with ...

a bucket full of treasures – lots of leaves, feathers, sticks, stones and even insects!

One day she
discovered some strange
blobs of jelly in the pond.

'What's THAT?' she said to Cassie.

Of course Cassie did not
answer – she is a dog!

She decided to ask Mum what these strange, blobby bubbles with tiny black dots were.

After all Mum knows EVERYTHING!

Lara took Mum to the pond. Mum smiled.
Then she explained what they were.

'Those are frogs' eggs - they're called
frogspawn.'

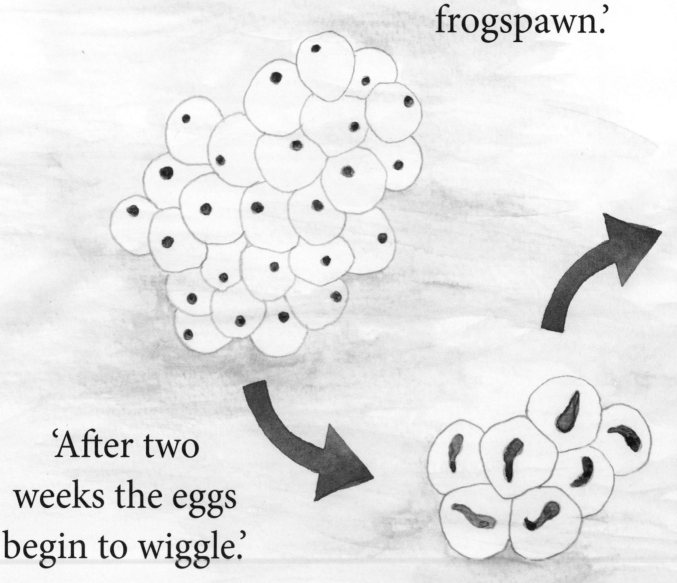

'After two
weeks the eggs
begin to wiggle.'

'Two weeks later the eggs turn into tadpoles that can swim.'

'After six weeks the tadpoles
grow back legs ...

and after eight weeks they
grow front legs too!'

'Their tails
become
shorter ...

and they turn
into a FROG!'

'So this is how jelly blobs with black dots develop into frogs.'

WOW! That means that in a few days time there will be loads of tiny frogs jumping around in my garden.

How COOL!!

But every time I go near the pond
they all hop away from me.

Maybe frogs don't like foxes?
I have an idea ...

It is fair to say
that Lara is HOPPING
MAD about frogs!